mc^2

DISCARD

$E = mc^2$

MW00905433

A Bad Case of the ALMOSTS

by
Janet Sumner Johnson

illustrated by
Alexandra Colombo

CAPSTONE EDITIONS
a capstone imprint

To London, who has the gift of seeing
almosts as opportunities. —J.S.J.

For all those who **almost** gave up fighting,
but finally did it. —A.C.

Published by Capstone Editions, an imprint of Capstone
1710 Roe Crest Drive, North Mankato, Minnesota 56003
capstonepub.com

Text copyright © 2023 Janet Sumner Johnson
Illustrations copyright © 2023 Alexandra Colombo

Library of Congress Cataloging-in-Publication Data is available on the Library of Congress website
ISBN: 9781684465378 (hardcover)

Summary: Abby is sick of almost getting things. It seems like the "almosts" rule her life!
But when she tackles the science fair, she finds out that the almosts aren't actually that bad.

Designed by Nathan Gassman

Printed and bound in China. PO5134

Abby had a bad case of the **ALMOSTS**.

At home, she **almost** beat her brother to the bathroom.

She **almost** got the last cookie.

At school, she **almost** got to be first in line.

She **almost** got 100 percent on her science test.

Almost even followed her to Science World!

She almost got sick on her favorite ride.

She was almost tall enough.

Maybe next time...

She almost had enough money.

"Almost, almost, almost!
It's **almost** every time!"

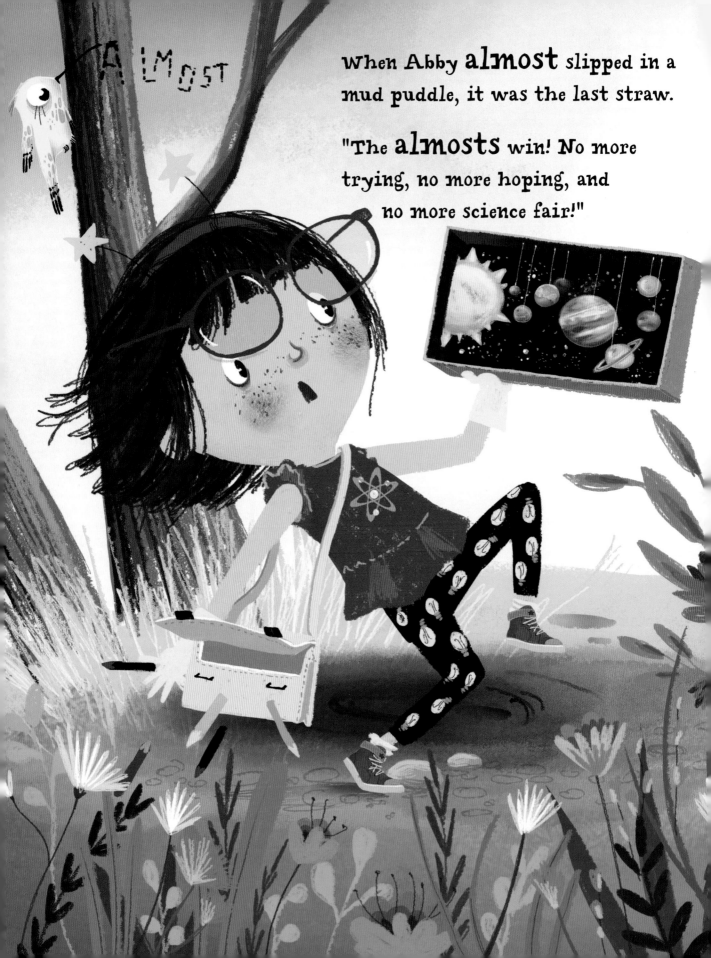

ALMOST

When Abby **almost** slipped in a mud puddle, it was the last straw.

"The **almosts** win! No more trying, no more hoping, and no more science fair!"

Abby **almost** threw her project straight into the trash when . . .

Are you okay? I **almost** fell in this exact same spot!

"Lucky you! **Almost** would have been nice," the girl replied.

Did that girl just say lucky? Could **almost** actually be a **good** thing?

When she got home, Abby decided to investigate.

At breakfast, Mom informed her they were **almost** out of Abby's favorite cereal.

Abby was about to write it under the bad column when Mom slid a full bowl in front of her.

At school, Abby **almost** got to complete the entire science project on her own.

Want a turn?

She **almost** earned
the star student prize.

At the store, Abby **almost** lost Pig!

Then she **almost** got a treat.

Maybe after your game...

At soccer, she **almost** got hit in the face.

Wow! That was close!

She **almost** scored a goal.

Awww!

Or was she?

Abby paused. "What if I'm only **almost** too scared?"
She closed her eyes, took a deep breath, and . . .

AND · · ·

AND · · ·

AND · · · ·

AND · · ·

AND · · ·

AND · · ·

Just to be sure, Abby tested out that **almost** a few more times. She even helped her brother!

But I'm too scared to jump!

What if you're only **almost** too scared?

That night, Abby studied her chart.

She definitely had a bad case of the **almosts**, but maybe that wasn't such a bad thing after all.

When her mom came in for storytime that night, Abby snuggled in.

"Wow! You're **almost** too big for my lap!" her mom said.

Abby grinned and snuggled closer.

"Thank goodness for **almosts**!"

Bad Almosts
- almost got 100%
- almost got to be 1 in the line

Good Almosts
- Almost out of favorite cereal
- Almost lost Pig
- Almost got hit in the face
- almost too scared
- almost fell
- almost quit the science fair

Conclusion:
THANK GOODNESS FOR ALMOSTS!!

THE DECISION TREE

Abby discovered that almosts can be both good and bad. Though we can't choose the almosts that pop up in our lives, we can choose our reactions. Start at the bottom and follow the decision tree arrows to see if your choices lead to sunshine or storms.

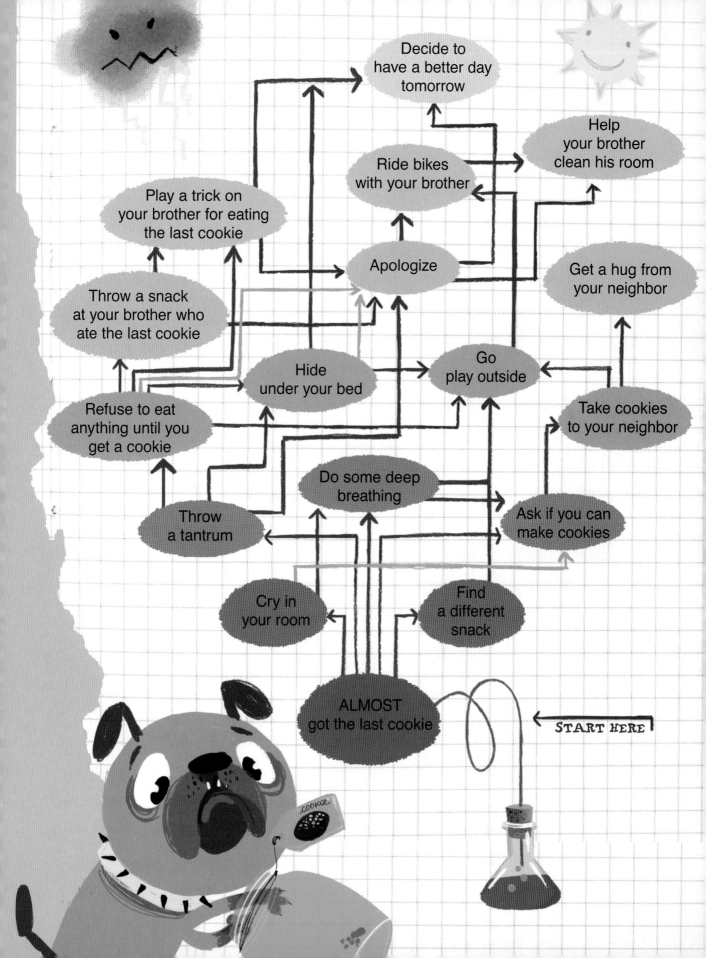

Janet Sumner Johnson lives in northern Utah with her husband, three kids, and a dog. She *almost* won her 3rd grade spelling bee. She *almost* got the solo in her 6th grade choir. And she *almost* convinced her family to move to the beach. When she's not writing, Janet loves eating cookies, laughing, and going on long walks. She is the author of *Help Wanted: Must Love Books* and *Braver Than Brave*. You can learn more about her at janetsumnerjohnson.com.

Alexandra Colombo's passion is writing and illustrating poems, fairy tales, and narrative picture book stories. She was born in Sofia, Bulgaria, and attended secondary school in Italy, specializing in scientific studies. She then studied at the Milan European Institute of Design, receiving a degree in illustration.